World of Fairy Tales

Beauty and the Beast
and
Jack and the Beanstalk

Two Tales and Their Histories

alphabet
soup

an imprint of

WINDMILL
BOOKS
New York

Published in 2010 by Windmill Books, LLC
303 Park Avenue South, Suite # 1280, New York, NY 10010-3657

Adaptations to North American Edition © 2010 Windmill Books

Copyright © 2010 Arcturus Publishing Ltd.

Editor (Arcturus): Carron Brown
Designer: Steve Flight

Library of Congress Cataloging-in-Publication Data

Brown, Carron.
    Beauty and the beast and Jack and the beanstalk: two tales and their histories / by Carron Brown. — 1st North American ed.
        p. cm. — (World of fairy tales)
    Summary: A retelling, accompanied by a brief history, of the two well-known tales in the first of which a young girl's great capacity to love overcomes the spell that turned a prince into a beast and, in the second, a young boy climbs a beanstalk where he outwits an ogre and makes his fortune.
    ISBN 978-1-60754-649-8 (library binding)—ISBN 978-1-60754-650-4 (pbk.)
    ISBN 978-1-60754-651-1 (6-pack)
    1. Fairy tales. [1. Fairy tales. 2. Folklore—France. 3. Folklore—England.] I. Beauty and the beast. English. II. Jack and the beanstalk. English. III. Title. IV. Title: Beauty and the beast and Jack and the beanstalk. V. Title: Jack and the beanstalk.
    PZ8.B697Be 2010
    [398.2]—dc22

2009036553

Printed in China

CPSIA Compliance Information: Batch #AW0102W: For further information contact Windmill Books, New York, New York at 1-866-478-0556.

For more great fiction and nonfiction, go to windmillbooks.com.

Beauty and the Beast

ONCE UPON A TIME, A RICH MERCHANT HAD three very beautiful daughters. The two older sisters were selfish and proud, but the youngest was so kind and sweet that everyone called her "Beauty." Every week, young men visited the merchant's house to ask to marry one of his three daughters. The two elder sisters replied that they would only marry a duke. As for Beauty, she said that she was too young and wanted to stay with her father for a while longer. Alas, one day the merchant lost all his fine possessions. He summoned his daughters and told them: "My poor children, all we have left is an old shack in the country. We shall have to go and live there."

The two elder sisters flew into a rage and stamped their feet—
their father was poor and there was nothing they could do. Soon,
they left for the country and Beauty did everything she could to help
her father. The hard work and fresh air made her even more beautiful.
One day, the merchant had to go to town for business.
The two elder sisters jumped for joy:
"Oh! Father, please bring us back some dresses and hats.
We've got nothing left to wear!" they cried.
The merchant promised, then he turned to Beauty
and asked her: "And how about you, Beauty?"
"Please bring me a rose, because roses do
not grow here," the girl replied softly.
Then the merchant hugged his
daughters and left for the town.

4

A few days later, the merchant rode home. Night fell as he was riding through a great dark forest in a storm, and he became lost. Suddenly, he saw a light shining in the distance. He gathered the last of his strength and set off through the storm toward the light. Soon, he arrived at a magnificent castle. The heavy door was open and inside, there was an strange silence.

"Hello? Is anyone there?" called the merchant.

But no one replied. He pushed open a door and entered a richly carpeted room hung with tapestries. There was a fire in the great fireplace, and a table was laid before it. Countless dishes laden with delicious food were set out before a single place setting. The merchant was starving so he could not resist.

"The lord of this castle will forgive my boldness," he said to himself as he started eating. Soon, midnight struck and still no one had appeared … Cautiously, the merchant began to explore the castle. He found a bedroom, lay down on the great bed, and fell into a deep sleep. Next morning, when he woke up, he found to his amazement that new clothes had been laid out for him on a chair, and a large breakfast had been placed on a table.

"Thank you, sir," said the merchant out loud to his invisible host, and sat down to eat.

Then, when he had eaten, the merchant prepared to leave.

As he passed a bush of bright red roses, he remembered his younger daughter and cut off the most beautiful branch for her. Suddenly, there was a sound like a thunderclap. The merchant turned around and found himself facing a horrible creature. Although he was dressed in elegant clothes, the monster had an enormous lion's head with huge sharp teeth. His great hairy paws had massive claws and his breath was harsh and fierce.

"Ungrateful man!" roared the Beast. "I saved your life and welcomed you into my castle. Now you steal what is most precious to me: my roses. Because of this, you will die, sir."

"My Lord, forgive me," begged the merchant. "I wanted to take these flowers to one of my daughters."

"Don't call me 'Lord'. My name is the Beast!" roared the monster. "But … you have daughters, you say? You can keep your life, as long as one of your daughters chooses to come here to die instead of you. If they refuse, you will come back. Otherwise my revenge will be terrible."

The poor man did not want to lose
one of his daughters, but at least he
was able to return and see them one last
time. So the merchant accepted and, with
a heavy heart, he went home. When he
arrived, his daughters ran to hug him. But
as he offered the roses to Beauty, he burst
into tears and said:

"Beauty, take these roses, they have cost
your poor father dearly!"

And he told them of his terrible adventure.
No sooner had he finished his story than
the two elder sisters turned on Beauty:

"Why didn't you ask for dresses, like we did?" they screamed. "Look what you have done: because of you, our father is going to die and you are not even sorry!"

"Crying is useless," replied Beauty. "Our father will not die. Since the Beast is willing for one of us to take our father's place, I will go to him."

The merchant pleaded and protested, but the girl would not change her mind. And so with sad farewells, she left her family. When she arrived at the castle, night had fallen and the huge building was plunged into a deep silence.

9

Beauty pushed open the door and went in. Immediately, the Beast appeared. Beauty thought she would die of terror. But the monster spoke to her in a voice that he tried to make sound gentle:

"I admire your courage. Follow me, I beg you. I will take you to your room."

When he had done so, the Beast bowed respectfully to Beauty and left.

"The Beast must have eaten already tonight. Tomorrow he will probably eat me," thought the girl before she fell asleep.

Next morning, Beauty decided to explore the castle. Although she was terrified of meeting the Beast at any moment, she could not help marveling at the splendor of the palace.

To her surprise, on one of the doors she read a sign that said: "Beauty's Drawing Room." She went in and found herself in the most beautiful room she had ever seen. A huge library filled a whole wall. Broad armchairs were set around a piano and a delicious breakfast was laid out. But above all, there were enormous bunches of red roses everywhere.

That evening, she found
the table laid for two in the great hall.
As she took her seat, the Beast appeared.
"Beauty, may I eat with you?" he asked her.
"You are the master," replied Beauty.
"No," replied the Beast, "you are the mistress here.
Tell me, you find me very ugly, don't you?"
Beauty, who never told lies, replied awkwardly:
"That's true. But I believe that you are good."
The monster did not reply. Then he took a mirror
out of his pocket and handed it to Beauty, saying:
"This is a magic mirror. You can see your family
in it any time you want."

Beauty took the mirror and saw her father standing in front of his shack. His eyes were filled with sorrow. Beauty was sad, but she thanked the Beast and felt less scared than before. Suddenly, he asked her another question:

"Beauty, would you agree to be my wife?"

Although she was worried about making him angry, Beauty replied trembling: "No, Beast."

"So farewell, Beauty," said the Beast sadly, as he left the room.

"Alas," Beauty wondered sadly, "why is he so ugly, when he seems so good? I couldn't possibly marry him. So it seems I must die!"

Time passed, and Beauty continued to live at the castle. She grew to like the Beast and discovered that he had a good heart. Soon Beauty forgot his terrifying ugliness, and every day she looked forward to dining together. Every evening the Beast asked Beauty if she would agree to marry him. The Beast's sadness made Beauty's heart ache and one evening she said to him:

"Beast, I will always be your friend, but I can't be your wife."

"Alright," replied the Beast, "but promise never to leave me."

Beauty was upset at his words. In her mirror she had seen that her father was now very ill.

"Beast, I long to see my father again. I shall be so unhappy if you won't allow me that joy," she begged.

"I don't want you to suffer," replied the Beast. "So go back to your father, even if I have to die of grief because I can't see you anymore. You can leave tomorrow. Take this ring. When you want to come back here, just lay it on a table. So, good-bye, Beauty."

Beauty promised to come back a week later, then she went up to bed. When she woke up next morning, she found she was already at her father's house. The poor merchant wept for joy to see his daughter. But her two sisters nearly choked with jealousy when they saw their sister so happy and even more beautiful than when she had left them. Together they decided to stop Beauty returning to the Beast.

"The monster will fly into a rage when he finds she has not kept her promise and he will take revenge on her," they said to one another.

When it was time for Beauty to leave, her sisters begged her to stay and Beauty agreed. But then Beauty saw the Beast in a dream. He was lying in the castle garden and he was dying. Realizing that she could not stay away, she put the ring on the table and went back to bed. When she woke up, she was back at the castle, but the Beast did not appear. Beauty remembered her dream and ran into the garden. She found the Beast lying on the grass and she hugged him, sobbing. Gently the Beast opened his eyes and said in a dying voice:

"Beauty, why didn't you keep your promise? I am dying because you didn't return."

"No, Beast, you won't die!" cried Beauty. "You are going to live and become my husband!"

Scarcely had Beauty spoken these words, when a flash of lightning struck the Beast. Beauty screamed in terror and hid her face. But when she opened her eyes again, instead of the Beast, she saw a young prince standing before her, who was incredibly handsome.

"Beauty," he said tenderly, "a witch cursed me to go about in the shape of a monster until a beautiful woman agreed to marry me. You alone were touched by my good heart and were able to overlook my ugliness."

Their wedding was celebrated the very next day. Thanks to the prince, Beauty's father's wealth was restored to him. As for her two sisters, they threw themselves at Beauty's feet and begged her forgiveness. And being very generous, she granted it.

Beauty lived for many years with the prince. They had many children and they were all very happy because their hearts were full of goodness.

THE END

Jack and the Beanstalk

ONCE UPON A TIME, IN A FAR AWAY COUNTRY, there lived a boy called Jack. He and his mother lived in a thatched cottage with a small garden. They worked hard, but were poor: all they had was a one old cow. One day she stopped giving them milk. So Jack's mother decided to sell the animal.

"Jack, the cow is no use to us any longer and she eats our hay. Tomorrow you will take her to market. She is not worth much, but try to get as good a price for her as you can."

Early next morning, Jack tied a rope around the cow's neck and took her to market.

On the way he met an old man dressed in rags, who was bent over a walking stick.

"Where are you going with that cow?" asked the old man.

"I'm going to the village to sell her," replied Jack.

"Well, you don't need to go all the way. If you like, I'll buy your cow. Look! In exchange I'll give you this bean. But take great care of it, because it's a magic bean! It will bring you riches and happiness, if you make good use of it," he told Jack.

Jack thought it over for a moment:

"Well, she's a very old cow and I'm afraid it will be difficult to sell her. I'm not risking much if I sell her to the old man. And perhaps I'll find a good way of using that bean!"

So Jack sold his cow for a bean, and hurried home, feeling quite happy with himself. When his mother saw him come in, she said:

"You are looking very pleased with yourself, my son. So, have you brought me lots of money?"

When she saw that all Jack had brought back was one small bean, the good woman flew into a rage.

"But what's going to happen to us? Why is my son so stupid? Go to your room! I don't want to see you again today!" she ordered him.

In her rage, she threw the bean out of the window, then she dropped onto a chair and burst into tears. Jack spent the rest of the day in his room, wishing he hadn't upset his mother so much. When evening came, he fell asleep.

The next morning, Jack got up to open the shutters. But try as he might with all his strength, he could not push them open. It was as if they were blocked on the outside. Jack ran into the yard to see what was in the way and there … oh, what a surprise! A gigantic beanstalk with huge leaves had grown up in the night, from the spot where the bean had fallen. The beanstalk was higher than the house; it went up higher and higher till its top was lost in the clouds.

"I am going to climb this beanstalk to see where it leads," Jack said to himself.

So, right away, he began climbing from branch
to branch and leaf to leaf.

He climbed for a long time, higher and higher.
He thought that soon he would touch the sky.
When he reached the top, among the clouds, he
saw a wide path bordered by trees.

Far off stood a magnificent castle.

Jack decided to go there.

When he arrived at the enormous castle door, Jack knocked. A giant of a woman opened the door to him.

"Good morning," he said politely. "I have come a long way and I am hungry and thirsty. Could you give me a glass of water and something to eat?"

"You would do better to leave at once," replied the woman. "My husband is a terrible ogre who eats children! If he finds you, he'll eat you with one mouthful!"

Suddenly the castle
began to shake.

"Quick! He's coming!
Hide!" said the woman.

Jack ran and hid.
Then he saw a huge
ogre with a cruel face
and pointed teeth. In one
hand he was carrying a
sack and in the other, a
sheep. The ogre threw the
sack into a corner and
some gold pieces fell out.
Suddenly, he stopped, his
nose twitched and he
began sniffing the air
in all directions.

"Fee, fie, foe, fum!
I smell fresh meat
here!" he cried, licking
his lips hungrily.

23

"It's that sheep you have just brought in. Give it to me and I'll cook it," replied his wife.

With a suspicious grunt, the ogre sat down in his huge chair and waited for the meal to be cooked. Then he flung himself greedily upon the sheep and ate it up, bones and all. Full at last, he went up to bed with his wife and began snoring so loudly that the whole castle shook.

24

Jack crept from his hiding place, took the sack full of gold pieces and ran away. The beanstalk was still there, and he slid down it to the ground. Jack's mother had been very worried by his disappearance and rushed out to greet him. He told her about his extraordinary adventure.

"You see, mother, it really was a magic bean. Look! This is for you," he said, giving her the sack full of gold pieces.

Jack's mother was thankful for having such a clever son. Both of them lived very well for a few months, thanks to the ogre's fortune.

When all the gold pieces had been spent, Jack decided to go back to the castle at the top of the beanstalk. He climbed from branch to branch and from leaf to leaf to the top of the magic plant. Once again, he knocked at the enormous castle door and begged the ogre's wife to let him in.

"You rascal! How dare you come back here? Last time you stole a sack full of gold pieces from us! Since then my husband has been in a very bad mood!"

But even before Jack could say a word in reply, the floor began to shake.

"Quick! Hide in the oven!" cried the woman.

Jack leapt through the door and ran to hide in the oven.

"Fee, fie, foe, fum! I smell fresh meat here!" shouted the ogre in a voice of thunder.

"It's that fat pig you have brought in. Give it to me, I'll cook it for you," replied his wife, quickly.

"Yes, I'd love some pork roasted in the oven," said the ogre.

"It will be much better roasted on the spit," his wife advised him.

Fortunately for Jack, the ogre agreed, and his wife roasted the pig on the spit in the fireplace. The hungry ogre swallowed the pig in one mouthful, bones and all.

26

When the ogre had finished his meal, he said to his wife:

"Bring me my hen!"

His wife came back with a little hen, which she put on the table.

"Lay an egg!" the ogre ordered the hen.

Jack was amazed to see the hen lay a golden egg! The ogre stroked the hen for a moment, then he yawned and fell asleep. Then Jack came out of his hiding place, picked up the hen, put her under his arm, and ran off from the castle as fast as his legs could carry him. Now Jack and his mother no longer had to worry about money because the hen laid a golden egg every day. But Jack began to find life boring, so he decided to return to the castle once more.

"Don't go, Jack. It's too dangerous," said his mother. But Jack took no notice. He climbed the beanstalk from branch to branch, from leaf to leaf. When he reached the top, he went to the castle. This time the heavy door was open. Jack slipped inside and reached the kitchen. Suddenly, the floor began to shake and the ogre strode into the room.

Panic-stricken, Jack looked around: where could he hide? Then he saw a big bowl full of soapy water, in which the giant's great socks were soaking. Without a moment's thought, he dived into the bowl. Poking his head out a little above the water, Jack saw the ogre stand still and begin to sniff the air:

"Fee, fie, foe, fum! I smell fresh meat here!" the ogre roared with a voice of thunder.

27

The ogre searched every corner of the kitchen. He opened all the cupboards, looked in the oven, behind the woodpile, then under the table, but he found nothing. Suddenly he went up to the bowl. Jack barely had time to draw his head back underwater before the ogre was peering into it. He began to sniff the bubbles suspiciously, but giants hate water and so the ogre did not plunge his hands into the bowl. With a disappointed grunt, he sat down at the table.

His meal was served and he began eating all the many dishes put in front of him. When he had finished, the ogre called to his wife:

"Bring me my harp," he roared.

His wife came back at once with a magnificent golden harp set with precious stones. She put it on the table and left the room.

"Play, golden harp," ordered the ogre in a loud voice.

Jack was amazed to hear the harp play a very sweet, sad tune all by itself, and lulled by the music, the ogre soon fell asleep.

Jack came out of his hiding place, grabbed the harp and made for the door. But he knocked the harp against the door-frame and its strings jangled. The sound woke the ogre and he gave a shout of rage that made the whole castle quake. He leapt to his feet and rushed off in pursuit of the thief. Jack ran as fast as he could, but the ogre ran after him with great strides and roaring:

"So it was you, you rascal! Beware when I catch you! This time you won't escape me!"

Jack jumped onto the beanstalk and slid all the way down to the bottom.

Behind him, the ogre clung to the beanstalk as well as he could and tried not to lose sight of the boy. But Jack was much too quick and agile and reached the ground well before him.

"Quick, mother, the ogre is coming! We must cut down the beanstalk," cried Jack.

With an axe and a saw, they both attacked the enormous stem. Suddenly there was a terrible crack and the entire beanstalk collapsed, crushing the giant who was just about to set foot on the ground.

From then on, Jack could never return to the castle. But, thanks to the hen that laid the golden eggs and the sweet music played by the magic harp, he lived for a long, happy time with his mother.

THE END

History of Beauty and the Beast

"Beauty and the Beast" is a traditional fairy tale that was first written down almost 450 years ago. Since that time, several versions of the story have been published with the most popular being by the 17th-century French author Charles Perrault.

However, it is only when the story written by another French author, called Madame Gabrielle-Suzanne Barbot de Villeneuve, was published in 1840 that the modern "Beauty and the Beast" tale is first recognized. In her version of the story, which was for adults, she wrote about the prince before he became the Beast. His father died when the prince was young and his mother, the queen, had to go to war to defend the kingdom. While she was away, the queen asked a fairy to look after the prince. However, the fairy was really an evil witch and it was she who turned him into the Beast. In her dreams, Beauty sees the Beast as he really is, but does not really understand that he has been cast under a spell until she marries him and he becomes the prince once more.

It is thought that Madame Villeneuve heard the fairy tale as a traditional oral (spoken not written) story that had existed in Europe for many years. It may have come originally from an ancient Greek tale.

The version of the story that we know today was printed only 16 years after Villeneuve's tale and is for younger readers. In the 19th century, the story began to be popular in France, England, and the United States.

Since then, "Beauty and Beast" has become a favorite fairy tale all over the world, and has been made into a ballet, theater productions, movies, books, and poems.

The story could have several meanings. Among them is that hard-working, kindhearted people may find the most happiness out of life—Beauty worked hard and was always generous and forgiving. Also, appearances can be misleading—the Beast wasn't really a monster, but a prince under a curse.

History of Jack and the Beanstalk

No one knows where or when the "Jack and the Beanstalk" tale first came into being, but it is believed it was originally told in England or in Germany, where there are many stories about giants. It was certainly spoken for centuries before it was finally written down. The first printed version was included in a book published in England in 1734 and was called *Enchantment demonstrated in the Story of Jack Spriggins and the Enchanted Bean*.

Various versions started to appear in print from the early 19th century onwards, with one called "The History of Jack and the Bean Stalk" by English publisher Benjamin Tabart in 1807. The version of the story that we know today was printed in 1890 in *English Fairy Tales* by a folklorist from Australia, called Joseph Jacobs. From then on, publishers mainly printed Jacobs' tale whenever they published a book of fairy tales, and so this version became the most popular.

The giant's "Fee, Fie, Foe, Fum!" saying appears in William Shakespeare's famous play "King Lear," which was written between 1603 and 1606. "Fie" is an old-fashioned word that was used to show disapproval. It was used in the language spoken around Shakespeare's time.

The wish to climb up into a rich and wonderful land way above the Earth is a common theme in legend and myth. Jack's beanstalk can be compared with the World Tree, which is a huge tree that supports the heavens in its upmost branches, with the Earth at the ground and an underworld in its roots. The World Tree is called Yggdrasil in Norse mythology.

"Jack and the Beanstalk" has grown popular from the time of its first printing, and has been made into a play and several films, as well as being reprinted countless times in many books.